CONVERSATIONS WITH AN ANGEL

An Extraordinary Love

LISA WILLIAMS
& ELIZABETH MEIER

BEYOND
PUBLISHING

Conversations With an Angel

Quantity sales special discounts are available on quantity purchases by corporations, associations, and others. For details, contact the publisher at the address above.

Orders by U.S. trade bookstores and wholesalers.
Email info@ BeyondPublishing.net

The Beyond Publishing Speakers Bureau can bring authors to your live event. For more information or to book an event contact the Beyond Publishing Speakers Bureau speak@BeyondPublishing.net

The Author can be reached directly at BeyondPublishing.net

Creative contribution by Ellen Walters, Jennifer Plaza and Carol McManus.

Cover Design - Low & Joe Creative, Brea, CA 92821

Illustrations - Marina Gonzales

Book Layout - DBree, StoneBear Design

Manufactured and printed in the United States of America distributed globally by BeyondPublishing.net

BEYOND PUBLISHING

New York | Los Angeles | London | Sydney

ISBN: 978-1-63792-138-8 Hardcover

ISBN: 978-1-63792-139-5 Paperback

Library of Congress Control Number: 2021919324

CONTENTS

PROLOGUE

The tough questions in life are often asked too late. For example, after a life-altering event such as a death, eyebrows are raised. Professionals seek answers, and loved ones vie for closure through autopsies, interviews, and the trip down memory lane as letters and books are scoured for a secret piece of a life moved on.

I felt a great loss when my best friend passed away from ovarian cancer. I struggled with wanting to be there for her while also shying away from asking questions that felt too invasive. And then the opportunity was gone and the questions I wished I had asked went unanswered. I wondered what was happening during that time where she lost consciousness and before she slipped away. I wondered even more what she was experiencing after she passed. Did she truly have no cares of this world? Did she miss the ones she left behind?

My friend Elizabeth's passing was a time of realization. I was blessed to have many days in the hospital with her through her 4+ year battle and I will treasure those conversations for the rest of my life. I will never forget the last visit. Her children were brought in to say good-bye, disbelief and denial etched on their faces. I knew they were hoping for a miracle so their prayers would be answered. We waited for the doctors to say those magic words, the variety of options they would suggest to ensure she could overcome yet again another complex issue related to her illness. Alas, this last time truly was the end. The words we had all wished to hear for so long, "You're truly in remission," never came, and her life slipped away. First, she lost consciousness, then her organs shut down. Finally, her heart beat for the last time and she took her final breath.

It seems that humans find the most difficult part of accepting death comes because our questions go unanswered. It is often a time of self-reflection. Did we show enough interest to ask the living the difficult questions? Did we talk about the fear and doubt we face when on death's door? Did we share our feelings about what awaits us on the other side?

Is it folly to believe that we go gently into that good night? What proof exists to say that after death we will experience the glory that we seek? From an early age, spiritual leaders lay the foundation of our moral upbringing and, depending on the belief system, that often includes the promise of some form of Heaven or pleasant afterlife.

Who is to say that the psychics who read Tarot cards, Angel cards, or those who act as mediums are wrong—or right? Are they charlatans? Is their jibber a ruse? Is there anyone among us who can prove otherwise? Skepticism is not proof. Interpretation is open to both believers and non-believers.

Why did the kings of old have Oracles or Mages serve in their courts? Who started the belief that there are guardian angels?

And who is right on the subject of what comes after death?

If the opportunity to ask someone in the afterlife were presented to you, what questions would you ask?

DEDICATION

My daughter Ciara asked my mom many times, Grammie, who's your best friend? My mom would say "oh Ciara Grace, I have many best friends!"

I too have been blessed with a few besties in my life but one, in particular, came along when God knew I needed an angel.

Elizabeth came into my life when I was truly in a pit of despair. Our friendship was one only God could have orchestrated. We were both in the unfortunate position of suddenly being thrust into the world of single parenthood with two little ones a piece, having found out that our husbands had each found love in the arms of another. I showed up to her house with a Bible in my hand and a prayer in my heart to join her single-parent Bible study. I was desperate for someone to really understand what I was going through as a scared, single mom. Boy, did God deliver when I met Elizabeth.

She taught me so much about grace and forgiveness during those early years of our friendship. She is one of the reasons I have such a great friendship with my ex-husband to this day...she told me I *had* to forgive him and most importantly I had to forgive myself for my part in the ending of my marriage. She helped me face my parts of the breakup that I came to realize after much soul-searching and counseling. (Thank God for good therapists and my pastors at Redhill Lutheran.)

What Elizabeth helped me learn during our early friendship was that "pit" I found myself in, was only a "place in time" and it too would pass. If I *chose* to work my way out. We were blessed to know one another during that period of falling in love again and yet knowing this time was different as we had two little lives that would both be impacted by the choice we were making to give our hearts away again.

One of the gifts Elizabeth had was making each of us feel like we were *her* special friend. She was a gifted listener. You could feel she really understood you. She was also not afraid to call you on your shit! One of the things I miss most about her is the calls to share and talk through the things we were struggling with: kids, blended marriage challenges, our sex lives, work woes, and the list goes on. We had an agreement to always be honest, even if it meant getting our egos wounded a bit. She was such a good sounding board. She let me vent too many times to count and then would always ask, "Are you asking for my advice or do you just need me to listen?" She was wise beyond her years and made me want to be a better me.

Elizabeth made me laugh so much. Sitting across from her for 8+ years with Kforce were some of my best days.

She had such a gift of words and sarcasm and that southern accent she managed to make a little stronger to charm her clients was infectious. What fun we had on our lovely girls' weekends away and all the fun book club parties.

When Elizabeth was diagnosed with ovarian cancer almost 5 years ago, she immediately went into warrior mode. She wore the armor of God until the day she died. The lives she touched at UCI oncology ward during her horrendous battle are too many to count. I remember when the cancer came back the first time and one of the first things she said to me was, "I guess God's not done with my missionary work at UCI yet." Wow!

Elizabeth had an amazing gift for words and I know I am not alone in remembering the many Caring Bridge posts she wrote that uplifted us and made us all laugh. This sweet woman, who was battling to keep meat on her bones, would write something that made us laugh and cry at the same time and was always anchored in her deep-seated faith in God's good plan.

Since I first met Elizabeth she talked about writing a book. The topics varied from blended families to the many sagas of our amazing book club. (Those alone could be made into a major motion picture!) She never got to write that book, so I decided to write one with her. Elizabeth and I shared a deep-seated belief and we both looked at life through the lens of beloved children of Jesus Christ. We also shared the belief that there are many beautiful things about all belief systems and that if only we could all strive to seek the commonalities in all of our faiths, how much happier this world would be. We both agreed...something is *real*! Shouldn't our story be about the life-long journey of discovering what that is for each of us?

Although Elizabeth didn't get the miracle of healing on this Earth that we were all praying desperately for, her legacy will go on in each of us. I know for the rest of my life I will ask myself, "What would Elizabeth say?" and think, "Elizabeth would love this!" I don't understand why her life was cut short, but what I do know is that she will continue to show up in each of our lives. God will continue to deliver, and I know from the depth of my soul that He can create something powerful from this horrible loss. I promised Elizabeth in my last day with her to be looking for those positive impacts every day. I promised her kids will continue to remember her and share memories of her. I promised to continue to talk about her and share her amazing life with others who may never have even met her.

It's never going to be the same without my sweet friend, but in this labor of love we are writing together, we will honor friendships everywhere and continue to celebrate life.

Elizabeth, I promise you will live on in the many ways you taught me how to love life and love unconditionally. You forever changed my life my darling friend, and I am so grateful to know with certainty I will see you again in eternity. You and mom better save some champagne for me!

CHAPTER 1
REUNITED

I was sitting at my vanity, on the soft black velvet stool. I'd finished brushing my hair when I noticed a pale blue haze in the reflection of the mirror. It caught my attention because I was readying myself for bed. It had been a tiring day, with both emotional and physical stressors pleading for my attention. I blinked slowly in an attempt to clear the haze and swiveled on the stool to face my bed.

"Hello?" I asked as if there would be anyone there.

To my horror, there was. But not to the likes of any being I knew. Instead, it was an apparition of sorts. The blue haze was seated on the edge of the bed. Her form solidified as I stared; a smile of disbelief paralyzed my face.

The female figure smiled back. The visage was reminiscent of my dearest friend and soulmate, Summer. I reached out to feel the translucent mass. As I suspected my hand disappeared in the haze, and I felt nothing. To say that I was in awe was an understatement.

She nodded to where I kept my journal. I slid off the stool and tip-toed to the desk, grabbed the small book with a pen, and edged back to the vanity. This time I did not sit.

She patted the bed beside her.

A sense of calm and trust enveloped me, and I went to sit beside the form. My fear gave way to wonder, and then questions. I had an overwhelming desire to fill myself with a flood of wisdom; wisdom for which I yearned and never knew I needed. I opened the book in hopes of my dear Angel communicating with me. I hoped that the burning questions that haunted me since she fell unconscious and passed would somehow be addressed.

She touched the book with her blue haze.

I seemed to know she wanted me to take the pen. My sweet friend laid her hand on mine, and I wrote.

Hello, Grace. My pen wrote the words, but they were not my thoughts.

I whimpered aloud. My best friend, sister by choice, was talking to me. But she'd been gone for seven months. What brought her presence before me now?

I asked, "How is this possible? I can't feel you, but I know you're here. You're sitting right beside me."

> I let you see me. You have felt me before but in a way that differs from what you know now. I marveled as the words poured onto the page.

"And this is the only way we can talk?" I asked.

She cupped my face in her hands and pressed her forehead to mine. There was a coolness that could have been my imagination or the sense of her being that made it so. I wasn't sure.

No, I wrote.

"Oh," I sighed. "Have you visited me before?"

Yes, I wrote.

For some reason, I was taken aback by that. But I thought better than to challenge this moment, cherishing the fact that my dearest friend never left, and she was here with me now. "How long have you been visiting me?"

Several months. The thought came through me in whispers. They were the kind of whispers that linger, not a fleeting voice but lyrical.

"So why couldn't I see you then? Why now?"

Because you are ready.

"Ready for what?"

To help you let me go.

"No, I screamed." I tried to latch onto the apparition. "No, you can't go. I have so much to say, so much to ask."

The blue haze intensified, solidifying her presence. It was human-like with Summer's blond and brown-eyed features.

I won't leave you, sweetie. You just won't need me.

"I'll always need you, darlin'. I miss you so much it hurts at times." Her odd response prompted my next question. "Do you miss me?"

Grace, there is more to us than what you see. I know you miss me, the way I used to be, but I am still here. I do miss you.

"What about Dave and the kids? Do you miss them?" She sighed with the emotion of someone more alive.

It's hard to describe exactly what I feel in a way you would understand. When it's said, "Set your mind on the things above, not on the things that are on Earth," what I can share is that I have been released of any worry of things here.

I miss you all. I would be lying if I said I did not. To watch the kids grow independent from the innocent babes they were delights me, but it's because I had a part in creating them.

She flopped back on the bed beside me, but the blanket did not waver or indent.

To say that I am happy is a misnomer. I loved being a mother. It's strange to watch them grow without my hugs and kisses. I never get to squeeze Amanda's hand when she needs encouragement. She goes to high school in the fall. We had plans. Will Carl remember the fresh biscuits I baked each Sunday? Do you know what it is like to watch your teenage son weep for you, his face pressed into his pillow, his hands clenched tight, while you can only stand there and watch?

The Earthly me would be torn apart. Yet I am blessed to instead watch their lives go by.

"I'm sorry, Summer. I hadn't thought about what you might miss. Everyone always talks about the dead being happy, surrounded by loved ones. It is when we get reunited. Is that not what happened with you?"

Yes, I met my mother. And when I crossed, she moved on. I expect that will happen with me, too. The angels are there to welcome us, just as they had at birth. It is a passing from one life unto the next. And with that life, you discover how much you did not know.

"Like what?"

She rolled to her side as she had in life when we would spend hours talking, sprawled across on my bed while I did coursework. I would have my back to the headboard, propped with pillows with her frame reaching across the queen-sized bed, stretched to all that was Summer.

Like how one becomes an Angel. And why you can't go back to talk to your family. There are rules. They are in place for the greater good, and although it does not make existing on the other side easier, it is wonderous. I will try to guide you, Grace. I am with you always. I am with my kids, too, but I am not meant to stay or interact. My energy will not manifest in their presence. As I am but energy, I cannot make myself known.

"Then why are you whispering to me rather than talking?"

Would this be more to your liking?

Her voice changed, becoming the true form of a ghost's whisper. It was the kind that caused the hairs on my arms to hurt and sent shivers through my spine.

"Ah, no. Please don't do that again," I pushed back, a bit quick on the request.

Then you know why I chose an internal dialogue. Be careful, for you are living and when you think on how you express yourself in your life, it is not possible for me in death. There is a reason they say the angels sing, Grace. My voice is high, and to many, is difficult to understand. But when I enter your thoughts, I manifest in body and voice. It is then that I join you. That I live on through you.

"Is it okay to ask questions? Can you answer them? I mean, is that allowed?"

Oh, it is allowed. And, as long as I am your angel you will feel my presence in each desire or warning. I have already offered my guidance. Do not be afraid to ask. It isn't every day you get to talk to your angel.

"Does everyone have an angel? Like a personal guide?"

You are referring to guardian angels. This is so much more, Grace. Put your pen aside. For now, lay back and think about what questions you have. And prepare for answers you do not want.

I tucked the pen in my journal to mark the page before I laid back on the bed and closed my eyes.

CHAPTER 2
THE ESSENCE OF TIME

I decided that if I was going to have a celestial visitor, then I needed to have the goods on hand to settle into a night of snacks. Just like when we had our chats on our girls' weekends every birthday of mine, a bottle of Cooks Extra Dry, cheese and fruit, and Godiva chocolate. I live with my hubby, daughter, and son. I wonder how I would explain this visit to Ben and the kids and decide for now to keep them just between us.

Who knows when she'll be back? I need to focus on my visitor and make her feel comfortable and welcome. I figure that if I recreate our old special chat times then perhaps, she will let go of what kept her emotions tied to her old life. I head to the store to pick up a few things I am missing.

That's my Grace, the high-pitched voice sung from the passenger seat. *Always overthinking.*

I swerved, an overreaction to Summer's voice beside me. Her blue haze manifested, and she was sitting in the passenger seat. A beam of sunlight streaming in the window formed rainbow hues as it struck the gray upholstery. The always-present dust particles drifted through her apparition. She was the sunshine with a familiar face. I brushed my hand through her. "You don't need to appear in the night?"

She shook her head, *No.*

It was astonishing. I thought visits from the afterlife were a nocturnal phenomenon. "I'm going grocery shopping." What else do you say to an angel that appears in the instant you're heading to the store?

For champagne and cheese from the sound of things. There is more than time as you know it, Grace.

"What do you mean? Like time on the clock or calendar?"

Yes and no. Time is created by man. It is a means to control events. Time synchronizes human lives in order to make it all make sense.

"What do you mean, make it all make sense? That we need time to keep us on track with our lives?"

No, I mean that time is immeasurable, that the human units are fallible. Look at how many versions of the calendar there have been. You are bound to the stress of time to the point that society expects one to know the exact minute of each day. For work schedules, school bus routes, appointments, and recorded time of death.

It is a legal obligation for the Death Certificate to have the hour, minutes, and seconds at which time the death occurred, documented on the certificate. After the deceased is celebrated with either a funeral or cremation, did it matter?

We are trained from an early age to celebrate the "firsts" in our lives. The first time our children roll over, the first time they crawl, stand, walk, run, ride a bike, go to school, have a boyfriend or girlfriend, learn to drive, have their heart broken, get married (hopefully only once, ha!), have our first grandchild. The list goes on. What about the celebrations of "the lasts?" The last time our children drank from a bottle, used a binkie, woke up in the middle of the night, took a bath with us, crept into our room because they were scared, let us hold their hand walking to school, gave us a big hug in front of all of their friends without a care in the world. One of my greatest desires for you would be to celebrate each moment as though it truly could be your last. How different would you live your life, Grace? It sounds so cliche, but are you truly living your "dash" in the best way possible?

I pulled into the grocery store's parking lot and chose a spot as far away from the store and other cars so I could talk. I was quite certain people would think I was using my phone. Still, it wasn't a conversation for others to overhear. "Honestly, Summer, I hear all the time not to sweat the small stuff and stop to smell the roses but until you and mom died in the span of 10 months and I suddenly lost my two best friends, I realized I was on a hamster wheel in my life. I was going through the motions in a lot of ways. Remember when I told you I looked in the mirror one day and I couldn't remember the last time I learned something new? When I started my business, I knew even you thought I was a little crazy. But since you got sick and then mom a few years later, I realized I better get moving on the bigger plan God had in store for me. I never thought much about the time of death. It was something I just accepted as necessary. I didn't realize it was recorded down to the seconds."

> And that is the truth of it, Grace. The recorded time does not matter to the one who has passed. The seconds and minutes are suggestions of measurements for moments in our lives. They are not actual. On this side, there is no month or day. Everything just is. We become part of it all.
>
> What surprised me most is that what we believed is not what is. Life is joyous, but only a part of what all living things are predestined for. On this side there is no schedule, no measurement, just an expanse of

wonder. I am more than the physical figure to which I was bound while living.

"Wait, what happened to you? I mean when you were in a coma it seemed like you heard me. And then when you passed it was peaceful. Do you remember any of those moments?" I tilted the seat back and concentrated on her sunlit figure.

I remember. You read the text messages and played the audio messages our girls sent you and sang to me. I remember when you spoke with the hospice nurse and she told you there were only hours left and you asked her, "can you please tell her husband that?" I remember the flurry of activity then when Carl brought the phone to my ear and my mom and brother said goodbye. I remember my sister made her flight to CA and within hours of her arriving at our house, I was gone. I fought letting go, letting go of what I knew. Life was safe and known, even with cancer and chemotherapy and radiation. But I also knew laughing, singing, rejoicing, and all the glories that come with life as we know it. I held on to the memories I created for future Christmases and birthdays. I did not realize that I was to become a part of something much greater–more fantastical.

She faced me from the seat and took my hand. The warm sunlight illuminated my skin and the light lingered over my fingers as they clenched the black shift knob. The light against the dark illuminated the semblance of her hand. I stared at it in awe. The sheer beauty of her light fascinated me. She may have visited the evening prior, but to me that moment in the car, sitting in the parking lot of the grocery store, was perfect and beautiful. For the first time in our encounter, I wept. It was not the kind of crying that takes your breath, but a silent stream of tears that became a pathway to the fabric of my blouse. My tears fell like spring raindrops. "What was it like...to die, I mean?"

She sat back; her form melted to the seat.

It was peaceful. I remember falling asleep–no noise or light, just sleep. And then, I do not know how long after, I opened my eyes. But there was more than sight. I heard the quiet and saw the blackness that, although was dark, had light. It was the true meaning of peace. There was nothing our human senses could grasp. I was in a waiting area where there was no sound, nothing to see, taste, touch, or smell. It was a freeing time that allowed me to let go. I was able to leave the world I had known behind me, and that was okay. I guess that is the biggest surprise. There was nothing and in that, there was everything.

It was as if the world did not exist. I had no thoughts and no plans. I was not happy, sad, or angry. My worries were behind me. The mental and physical hurt did not exist. Yet, I was still me. Does that make sense?

"Maybe? I always wondered what it would be like. To wake on the other side, reborn into our new role. But I never thought about it being nothing." I wasn't feeling like cheese and fruit anymore and headed to the In and Out near my house for a burger, fries, and a chocolate shake. Discussing the afterlife and what awaits was more than the sister chats we shared in the past. It was real, and I wanted and thought I needed to have something substantial to anchor me to the moment. Flavors from hot summer days, salty and sweet, were the comfort foods I craved. While I waited in the line of cars, her explanations unfolded and I wondered if there was not a hidden lesson. I think she was telling me to enjoy life now, while it was here. If that wasn't the message, then at least I would have a tasty meal while learning secrets I doubted anyone else on Earth knew or could access.

Liminal space, that's what it is, Grace. It's where there is no purpose but being. It is a transition that forms us into an accepting force. But that's the beauty of all that is. We believed with all our might that we would live on, but the vastness of what we become is indescribable. There is no limit to the universe and therefore no limit to us. We are the energy that joins what is and what becomes. I am here but in time I too will pass to the next phase of my being. Therefore, I await my next transition.

People spend their lives worrying about the moment of death. The when, where, and how are questions most humans grapple with. It is less about the anticipation of the transition, but for fear of change. If we celebrate our lives while we live, then the life will be celebrated when we leave. And the reflection we incur during our time in the liminal space will offer us peace.

I am at peace. Since I manifested and have given myself to you, to speak with you, I feel that my human emotions are becoming a memory. The weight of sadness from my illness and the thoughts of leaving those I love behind have been lifted. I love my family, Grace, but there is another calling–a pull to become as one with the next.

"I am here for you, Summer." I pulled forward to the drive-thru window and ordered. While I waited for my food, a thought occurred to me. "You have to let go. Your children will never forget who you are and the life you led. They will cherish their memories of you. We know that a mother's love is like no other, and you made your mark. When they close their eyes at night, they can feel your arms and kisses. They will move forward and heal from your loss with those memories as a guide. You must do the same."

I handed the cash to the woman at the window and took my meal, then drove back to my California bungalow and patch of green yard. Before Summer's visit, it seemed to be the brightest part of my home in the sunlight. But Summer was opening my eyes to what light I may yet experience. I paused on my brick steps to look back over the lawn. Each blade of grass swayed in the soft breeze. The breeze itself was a realization that there was so much I could not see yet knew was there. The dandelions danced and my wind chime clanged with soft strikes on the tubes by the wooden clapper. It was tranquil and what I had imagined my time in liminal space would have been. But now, I was lost in the thought of one day becoming an angel myself. An angel that would visit and enlighten the lucky soul to which I would be linked.

I left the car with Summer behind me but when I turned, she was waiting at the bottom of the steps for me to enter the house. It was a quiet welcome, but not in an ominous way. It was the first quiet peace I'd felt in months. Somehow, in an afternoon, learning about what awaits lifted my worry and the profound sense of her loss.

I opened the door and motioned for her to pass. Instead, she paused in front of me, touched my cheek, and evaporated. The vision that was her became a haze of pale blues and yellows. As the light dissipated the breeze grew stronger. The chimes clanged a little louder and she was gone. But I didn't feel sad. I knew I would see her again, perhaps tomorrow or not, but it didn't matter. I took the shake and the white paper bag holding my splurge of a dinner to the sofa. Ben was at the golf course and the kids all had sleepovers with friends, so I knew I had the house to myself for a bit. I turned on the TV and smiled in the calm that came from learning and knowing. And in that moment, I was content. I started with the chocolate shake and flicked through the channels embracing the feeling of contentment for the first time since her passing.

CHAPTER 3
WHY ARE WE HERE?

Three months went by since my angel visit. The leaves were changing colors to showcase the transition of the bright green of summer to the gold of autumn. I approached my new thoughts with wonder. There was liminal space in all that was to be. It was profound. And to know that Summer was a part of that, that we were all a part of that, allowed me to appreciate every moment in the here and now. I was acutely aware that here and now could be gone in an instant.

When I stepped back to reflect on time as a whole and how many transitions had taken place, plus those yet to come, it was phenomenal to me. The weeks rolled by, and in my head, I no longer expected her to reappear. I was sad at first because she never said goodbye. But in my heart, I figured it was only a matter of time, human time, until she came again.

In the meantime, I took advantage of knowing that I could ask questions and receive answers. I kept that journal and pen together as a special memento of Summer's first visit, but also to write those questions. They were always at the ready, in my purse or on my nightstand. My angel had changed my life in a way that gave me pause and time to reflect. I could only imagine what new insights I was bound to learn from our next meeting.

I made a big decision after her first visit. I decided to officially adopt a "no a-holes" rule! I decided to stop working for a-holes, with a-holes, and to no longer serve a-holes in my life. I had been doing a business on the side that I absolutely loved and yet had continued to be bound by the golden handcuffs of my corporate exec role. One day, I'd come home from work tired and weary. I was bringing home the same complaints to my hubby and kids that I had for a few years and taking no action to change that circumstance.

I wrote down a question for the next time she came to visit. "What would Summer do?" Then I realized I knew exactly what she would tell me. *What are you waiting for? It's about time!*

The next day, I was scheduled to go home to visit my folks in Alaska. Mom had been battling cancer for about 6 months at this point, and I was so blessed to have the means to visit her often but also the tenure at my job to have accrued generous vacation time. I used every drop I had during those 10 months of my mom's battle.

I was on my 19th boss in twenty-two years and this one was a real doozy. He put me on "a plan," and I started to realize my time may be limited in this corporate gig. I know "ageism" is a real thing, but at nearly forty-eight, I thought I was being caught up in "experiencism." There were a lot of young people they could hire for much less than they were paying me. Put them on a low salary and low commission, and they would fall in line with the corporate party line and give them no BS.

On my layover in Seattle, I called my hubby, Ben, and told him, "Babe, I'm not going back! Mom doesn't have long and I'm going to take the next few months off and cherish these last moments. I see the end of my corporate career fast approaching."

About 3 months after Summer's first visit, while I slept, I dreamt of floating in the vast openness that is our universe. I was surrounded by blackness and distant glints of stars. Summer was there, in my thoughts and I listened to her humming. I could not make out the tune, but it was soft and calming. I was weightless and free. A wonderful feeling after a long day. In my dream, I couldn't even remember what made the day so tiring. My dream took all my cares away, and once again, I was reunited with my best friend and soulmate.

"Hello, Summer," I said.

Hello, Grace.

"I haven't seen you for a while. Are you okay? I mean that as in how you are doing, not a casual greeting." My joy in having her back turned to concern as I remembered the part about her having to let go and resisting. I could sense the bits of the mother she was still having a hold on her. But it was three months for me, so perhaps it wasn't so long for her. I repeated, "Are you okay?"

> I am. For as long as I have been away from you, I have learned. You've seen pictures of the Milky Way and other galaxies. There are an infinite number of them, and they are all energy. I am a part of all of that, not just here with you, but in the sun, moon, stars, and beyond. When I say we are all a part of it, it is true.

"We used to talk under the stars. Remember, Summer?" I asked the figure in my dream. "You made coffee and we'd wrapped ourselves in plush blankets to watch the stars from our canvas camping chairs on clear summer nights. I loved those moments and cherished those memories."

She peered around my dream, not keeping her focus on anything in particular. Her form seemed to pulse like a flashlight whose bulb and battery are at odds. First, the light brightens and then it dims, it flickers, and brightens again. Her haze did the same but in a pulsating rhythm. Even in my dream, I was determined to find out what this had to do with her state.

"Why are we here, Summer?"

> I wish to show you. When we pass, we are freed. Our souls, spirits, or whatever you choose to call

them are no longer contained. The beauty you see in the world and here in our universe is made from our signature. We cannot be destroyed, for we are what is. I was surprised to learn there is no Being in charge. The creator of us all is the creator of all that is. And we are destined to become one with that. I am an angel, but it is a transitional stage. That is why you see my form. It is what is left of me from my humanity. The haze is the release of my energy. When the light that is me grows, and the resemblance that is me fades, then I will have completed my transition.

"Then you are okay."

Yes, I am okay, Grace. I am enamored with my new life and await the day that I become a piece of the whole, a part of the expanse. My sadness is no more, my children are healing. I truly have no cares of this world as you know it. I have learned that I am able to share my energy with them as they sleep.

A transference of interpersonal energy is a way of sharing one's energy with other living and nonliving things. Vibrations are caused by energy. The ebb and flow of a current is felt by all of us. Even I feel your energy as I visit you. My children feel my energy when I am near, and I give them a part of me. They are unaware of the transference, but it is not possible for two beings or objects to not share. So, as my time away from my humanity grows, my energy reaches out to more places. I use that to give that bit of myself to them. And in doing so, I have helped them to heal. Their sadness has eased. I no longer feel the emotions I had as a human. I am in awe, as you believe you have been.

When you open yourself to this new phase of existence, you realize how small your piece of humanity was. And as you visit loved ones, you see them in their mourning. But the pull to evolve is too strong to keep you tethered to the old life you were forced to leave behind.

It is contentment. It is peace.

"You've been visiting the kids? Do they know? Have they seen you?" I felt animated in that dark expanse within my dream. "Am I dreaming?"

It is in dreams that I am able to visit with the kids, but they do not know I am there. They believe, as you did, that I was a memory, a fading form to grasp the image of in the early morning light upon awakening. For awakening from a visit is energizing.

A good dream or visit often leaves them with a sense of calm just as you feel now. You will awaken, fix dinner, and settle in. There are signs that your loved ones have visited. Look for currents that make you feel their presence, even though you cannot see them. It's like the energy you feel sometimes when you touch a photo. It is picked up by the camera but not by the naked eye.

Why be skeptical of the interpersonal energy exchange if you are accepting of other forms? Might I say the warmth of a hot summer's day is a transference of the sun's energy? It cannot be seen, but you can feel it. It bakes the ground and causes temperatures to rise. But have you ever seen the heat? That wiggly wave of air above a heated surface is the result of the heat, not the heat itself. The actual heat is not visible, and the interpersonal energy transference is no different. There is no way to prove or disprove its existence and therefore it is met with skepticism, for the simple fact that it cannot be proved. At what point, I wonder, will society accept what cannot be proved until it is disproved?

"You're talking about faith, aren't you?" I pondered the idea that faith had nothing to do with religion and everything to do with acceptance. Humans have trouble accepting things they are incapable of explaining. They hide their "acceptance secret" from the world, for simple vanity.

> Grace, having faith does mean believing. But it means believing in what you feel, and yes that can be tangible or metaphysical. There are vibes people associate with new encounters and situations. We speak of chemistry between two potential partners, and we talk of faith as a synonym for trust. The moment I passed from my human life, I was faced with an enigma, perhaps the greatest one of all. It was the realization that there is a piece of me in all that is. I learned that the kids and you carry on my energy in your living lives. And when you cross over, that energy will touch others.
>
> It touches others now. You had endless days of frustration at work and you were bringing that home to Ben and the kids. Now that you have "hired yourself" as you like to say, your energy has shifted to a more positive plane, one that is pulsating in a different vibration entirely. You may find that you actually repel some of those closest to you that haven't also evolved into a more energized vibration. You have started the process of becoming a higher

energy person in your circle. When a person with positive light and energy meets another with positive light and energy, positive things happen. You need to continue to find like-minded people to lock arms with and involve them with your business. They will feed your energy and you will feed theirs. As you continue to evolve you may find the "energy vampires" in your life are easier to let go of. It doesn't mean you don't love them, but if you are going to accomplish the things I believe God has meant for you to accomplish, you will spend less and less time with them.

"I know what you're saying. There are people I worked with who seemed to drain the life out of me. Oh, man, Mike and Linda were just two." My dream shifted to one of the last scenes at the office before I resigned. Mike was lecturing the office on how disappointed he was that the client recapture calls were not productive today. He reminded us it was our responsibility to bring back old clients. Then Linda started complaining about the people using the coffee machine in the breakroom and how it was a violation of company policy. She referred to the employee manual that all appliances must be supplied by the employer. The meeting resulted in a verbal skirmish that ended with one coworker threatening to take her coffee maker home, and another who swore she would bring their own because she was not going to work without coffee. Mike relented and said they could have a coffee maker, so Linda called corporate. Corporate got on a Zoom call advising everyone that all appliances violated the terms of their insurance.

In the end, Mike read the policy to the employees that only water bottles were allowed. Any preparation or consumption of food or drink must be done off premises and only during lunch or scheduled breaks. He ended the meeting by doubling the number of calls each person was expected to make to recapture lost clients. I groaned in my sleep knowing I had to make thirty calls before the end of my shift, in addition to my other duties and projects.

"Yeah, I know what you mean. Some people suck the life out of you." Just from petty issues and unrealistic expectations. I am making myself less and less available for them the deeper I grow into my own God-gifted life. I heard something the other day that struck me to the core. "Do not take offense, no matter how big or small. To do so only serves to weaken ones character." The more I have embraced this concept, the more I can just laugh at these encounters.

Life is beautiful, Grace, whether you are living or not. I promise we were never meant to be bound to a monotonous routine such as long workdays that offer no reward. Happiness builds energy. That is why you find beauty in nature and all Earth's creatures. Enjoy it. Savor it. Don't let two humans like Mike and Linda destroy your vision of the splendor of life. One day they will learn as you and I have, that a coffee maker in the breakroom and phone call quotas never mattered.

"Speaking of Earth's creatures, this may seem silly to ask but are there any of our pets on the other side? Sometimes I think Ben may be more excited to see Logan in heaven than I am! What about family? You spoke of your mother, but what about other family members? You never answered."

CHAPTER 4
ENERGY THAT CONNECTS

Summer had evaded my direct questions during the last two encounters. In life, she would have answered them. She was a matter-of-fact individual who had no qualms about sharing her thoughts and opinions. But the longer she spent as an angel, the more removed she became from her old human life. I awoke from that odd dream shortly after I posed two questions. "Are there any of our pets on the other side?" and "You spoke of your mother, but what about other family members?"

It was a good four months before our next visit. This time I seemed to expect her, like an 'Oh, there you are' kind of thing. I was reading in my bed in the warm yellow glow of two brass table lamps. They accented my brass bed frame and blended with the white walls with rosebud border. It was winter, so I was tucked under my white duvet, wearing my Christmas pajamas. The pink plaid matched the color of the roses on the border.

Summer appeared above me, her haze drifted down from the ceiling and settled on the empty side of my queen bed.

"Hey," I said.

How have you been, Grace?

"I'm usually the one asking questions," I laughed. "I'm actually really good. I'm excited about life. There are days that I wake up absolutely terrified of the fact that I left my corporate career, but when I think about the things I am learning and the people I am blessed to be working with, I can't believe I waited this long. I didn't realize how truly unfulfilled I was until I was gone. I have been wondering when I'd get to see you again. I have so many questions."

> As I said, time is different in the afterlife. Do you have your questions? In your little book?

I fumbled with the nightstand drawer and swapped the book I was reading for the journal where I'd recorded a log of new questions. I had plenty of time to think about the answers my dear friend provided during prior visits. There were no 'yes' or 'no' replies. They were long-winded explanations. Perhaps there was no such thing as simple affirmative or negative summations in the afterlife.

I worked hard to find other ways to ask my questions. Seeking guidance from an angel was not unheard of, however, the way to receive their responses might differ. "Summer, how can I ensure you and my family will be there with me when my time comes? Is there more I should be doing here on Earth that will ensure that happens?" Cryptic, maybe, but who doesn't want to know if our loved ones are on the other side.

Look around, Grace. They await and transition on in our passing. I await your time and will transition to become one with the universe. My energy will merge with the sun and all that is. When my children pass, I will greet them before returning to my greater state. All creatures are a part of life and existence. What you have chosen not to ask is 'Do I know when or how your end will come?' But I am not a fortune teller, I am a guide to watch over you so that you make decisions that better your life. The best way I am able is to visit in a manifested form. You are healing from my loss, though you do not yet see you did not lose me. When I passed, my energy was directed to my waiting self. At your Earthly life's end, you will join me. That is all I am able to disclose.

I swallowed. Was that a prediction of my end? It warmed me to know that I would not die alone. She was right; it was a big question I did not want to ask. "So, then if angels are fluid in their form, how do they move on? I want to be there for my children and husband."

Walk with me, Grace.

***

I snuck past my children's bedrooms. Though they were in their teens, I walked with caution so as not to disturb them.

Chances were good it was for nothing because they would have their earbuds in place, absorbed by Youtube or Tik Tok. My husband, Ben, was working. He had worked nights ever since my son was born, fourteen years ago. But hospitals never closed, and he was an essential worker. It made Summer's visits welcome because I did get tired of being alone.

I tip-toed until we passed their doors, then slipped down the staircase. I pulled on my dark brown UGGs with the cream-colored fur and draped my down coat over my shoulders as we headed outside under the moonlit sky.

The crab apple tree in the front yard had a fresh layer of snow that frosted its branches. The quiet of the sparkling winter night and Summer's haze reminded me of Cinderella and her fairy godmother. *How beautiful,* I thought. It was as though Summer was my very own fairy godmother. She would be with me until my final day, and I never knew when to expect her.

She settled next to me as I stood on the crisp snow-covered steps and absorbed the wonder before us. The glittering snow twinkled in the moonlight. Her earlier words played through my mind—*we are all a part of the whole.*

"Is it wrong to think that each snowflake is a piece of someone's heart, their loved one's soul?" I reached down to feel the soft powder and watched it melt in my hands. "That energy you talk about created the heat that melted the snow in my hand?"

Grace, our loved ones, and yes even our pets are energy, too. They are energy bound into tiny cells and built into every being by a creator. Their consciousness, ours if you will, is part of that energy which we can re-collect. The act of re-collecting leads to our memories that surface. Those memories are the energy that those loved ones imprinted on us before they moved on. Their transitions did not change. They are there to greet us in the subconscious collection upon our crossing. The love that we share as humans is a manifestation of energy that mingles with that of another.

We as humans recognize the familiar energy. Those energies grow stronger with each encounter because of the interpersonal exchange and that causes our loved ones to recognize our energy when we emerge from the liminal space.

"I'm confused. Are you saying that we call our loved ones to us after death?"

In a way, yes. Think of it as they sense your energy and follow the draw. How do you think your dog knows when you are driving home and on your street? It is its energy that bonded with yours and created that unconditional love. It is programmed into your dog's energy, so it is drawn to what it knows.

When we pass on, our energies act as a magnet to the energy of those we leave behind, having a stronger pull between those of close relationships.

I tapped at a bit of snow, compacting it with the toe of my boot. I marveled at the thought of thousands of snowflakes I patted sticking together. Later, they would melt together and evaporate. I was starting to see the bigger picture. At least I hoped that I was on the right track. "If you remember, we used to talk about our ancestors and whether they would be on the other side."

There are some cultures that believed, and still believe, that the stars in the night were their ancestors watching over them. In one respect, they are correct. When you die, your physical body stops producing energy, and the energy that is within goes on to the liminal space. You wait for your consciousness to awaken, reborn, and that awareness during the transition calls to familiar energy. That call is your non-physical self that seeks the familiar. We leave the familiar behind, but going forth to our angelic self, we are drawn to older familiar signatures. Those familiar signatures have imprinted with even older signatures as they held relationships in their human lives.

"So, our ancestors are a part of the stars in the sky, and all that is around us. Their love is part of the chain that connects us in the afterlife." I smiled, both in awe of the grand idea, but also in no longer mourning my friend. I was able to celebrate the fact that death was not a loss, but a continuation of a whole—a rejoining and reconnection. "Hey, Summer, if you are an angel, and I can see you, then are there angels all around us?"

There are, but we do not stay. Our energy is called, and we follow. At times I am with my children and husband. Other times, I am everywhere. Appreciate what you see. Enjoy each sun-filled day, splash in a rain puddle. It is energy and life that created it all, and those who passed on have become a part of it all. That old cliche "pause to smell the roses" is a literal manifestation of our loved ones visiting us in their energetic form. If only more people would actually pause long enough. I wish this for you, Grace.

A set of headlights rounded the bend on my rural street. I watched as its tires left tracks in the snow proving the vehicle was there, even though it was no longer in that same spot.

It was my husband. He had been on the road at another point and now was here. I was connecting the idea Summer presented. From the time the car was at the bend to when it was pulling in the driveway, it left a signature in the snow. And the fact that my husband drove home to the kids and me without a physical connection proved that love was our bond. It was an invisible bond that formed a desire within the living to reconnect with that mutual energy. Perhaps that is why children say, 'I want my mommy', or people from around the globe say, 'I just want to go home'.

My husband pulled into the garage, and I slipped inside the door to take off my boots and coat. I never waited for him to come home; he just did, and we resumed our routine. But perhaps Summer was trying to teach me a lesson. I wanted to show my appreciation to the love of my life for returning to me, to us.

I raced to the kitchen to fix a chicken sandwich and glass of milk for him before he came in from the garage. His routine was to place his boots by the door, grab his duffel bag, and set the alarm.

Just as he came through the door, I was adding a chocolate chip cookie to the small sandwich plate. His arms wound around me, and I could feel the questioning in his embrace.

"You know I love you, right?" I asked.

He pulled back to look in my eyes. "I love you, more."

CHAPTER 5
WHEN LIFE FADES

Another six months went by and no visit from Summer. Under the warm summer sun, the birds were chirping and the clear blue sky let the purple hue of the distant mountains stand in glory. The lyrics of "America the Beautiful" filled my mind. They were as true as the day they were written. I was staring at the fields of grain in the flats before the mountainous backdrop.

Even though my kids were teens and liked their time to be their own, we continued the tradition of strawberry picking at the farms that stretched along in the mountain shadows. I brought wicker baskets for each of us to fill under the spacious skies and thought about that song again. It was the time of year when flags decorated fences and porch fronts.

Picking strawberries was a tradition for folks all around. This was family time to enjoy activities beyond technology. There were children running up and down the rows of strawberries and parents carrying infants in pouches. Grandparents used canes to point at plump red berries for the little smiling sun-kissed faces to pick.

We walked along, my kids still play-fighting and pretending to throw berries at one another, then bumping arms in a display of sibling love. I led the way further from the entrance so we could get to the less picked-over plants. Most of the visitors stayed near the parking lot. I noticed only one mom, perhaps a grandma, and young boy in the area where we were headed, and I doubted they could pick many strawberries with their one small basket.

As I neared, I saw that she had an oxygen tank slung over her shoulder. She carried the small basket in her frail hands. The boy would pick a berry and show it to her before dropping it in the basket. She rewarded him with a smile for every berry. I wondered if it was her way of showing her pride and love for the boy, wanting to make sure it was enough to last for a lifetime. I wasn't sure if it was her son or her grandson.

I walked a bit closer, my heart raced as a sinking feeling settled in my belly. In that instant, I knew the pain the boy was feeling. I knew it because when my mother passed, it tore me to pieces. The boy did not run but walked back and forth to the woman.

"Grandma, look at this one," the boy called as he approached her. The double berry looked huge in his small hands.

The woman smiled and patted him on the head, the sparkle of unshed tears affirmed her love for the boy. She attempted a deep breath and the machine whirred. The tube beneath her nose slid along her upper lip from perspiration.

She readjusted it and tucked the tubing behind her ears.

My kids raced ahead down two separate rows of strawberries, challenging each other to fill their baskets first. My husband followed in the third row carrying a basket of his own.

I walked over to the woman. "Excuse me."

"Oh, hello," she coughed in a hoarse whisper.

"He's a handsome one," I tilted my head toward her grandson.

She smiled and nodded.

"May I ask, what–" my eyes drifted to the oxygen tank.

"COPD," she said.

"Ah. Is there anything I can do?"

"Not unless you have a spare set of lungs in your pocket. I'm on the list." Her smile lit up her face when the boy returned with more berries to drop in the basket. He scurried off before she continued, "He's never known me not to have the Grammy Air." She patted the machine in her bag.

"I like the name," I smiled.

"Thanks," she shook her head, "but between you and me, I wish I didn't need it."

I didn't know what to say after that. Disease caused pain and suffering to the living. That included all the living; the patient, the family, and the doctors and nurses with their hands tied or no cure to make it better.

I wondered why disease had to exist. It wasn't fair or right for good people to suffer.

The familiar blue haze appeared behind the woman. Startled, I took a step back. I never had a visit from Summer in front of other people. "I'm sorry," I said to the woman. "I hope something comes through for you soon."

"It is what it is," she sighed. "I just want my grandson to remember me." Her eyes glinted.

The blue haze formed into Summer. The woman didn't seem to notice. She held her basket out as her grandson returned with a giant strawberry. I walked far enough away to be out of earshot.

"You came back," I whispered.

You called.

"What?"

This woman reminded you of me. Your memories of the hours before my passing made your heart race. Our energy was entwined in life. I feel you, Grace. Those memories are visits from the past. When you grieve, know that the heaviness in your chest knows mine. That is the call, Grace.

"Grammie, I got the biggest one," the boy shouted from behind me. "Grammie?" his voice sounded smaller.

I turned around to look. My husband and kids were rushing toward the little boy.

The woman lay at the edge of the strawberry patch, her grandson picking up the strawberries scattered around her. He put them back in the basket. "Grammie, you dropped these." He squatted next to her and touched her blue-gray hair. "Grammie?"

"Oh no, Summer. Tell me she's not... Oh, that poor boy." I rushed back to the spot where the woman lay. Summer's haze manifested into the life-size friend I remembered, not solid but fully visible. She stayed at my side. "Did anyone call 911?" I shouted.

My husband was on his phone just as a man wearing a fireman's T-shirt raced up. He gave the basket of berries to the little boy and told him to go the farmer's stand and send another grown-up back to help. "You stay there. We'll take care of your grandma."

Tears were streaming down the little boy's face as he ran off.

Guys," I yelled to my kids. "Go with him. Tell them she has COPD and collapsed."

My kids took off after the little boy, carrying their baskets of fresh-picked strawberries. They were supposed to be delicious, sweet juicy reminders of a special day. Now the sting of a heartless disease bore down on them, too. Strawberry shortcakes and bowls full of berries and cream would always be a reminder of this random event.

The berry-picking families had gathered around the fallen woman. A young man, maybe in his late twenties, came running from the market. "Mom?" he called. He knelt beside her and held her hand. "Hold on. Help is on the way."

The man with the fireman's t-shirt smiled as he nodded. "Her pulse is weak, but she's with us."

I breathed a sigh of relief and backed away from the crowd. "Summer, explain to me why things like this happen? Why is there disease and hurt? Why is there pain?" I wiped my falling tears with the back of my hand.

> Disease is a part of life, Grace. We are meant to transition. At what time or in what way is not determined. It is what happens when we pass that matters most. How many hearts did we touch? The mingling of energy that allows our memories to re-collect those signatures and the manifestation of our strengthened bonds means that our lives were lived good and well.
>
> Disease is a means to building relationships, sharing energy, innovation, and invention. It brings people together. True, it is an awful part of life. It hurts in many ways, but that pain leads to treatments and cures. Many of those creations were because of painful memories. How many times have you heard

a young person say they wanted to be a doctor to help people that were sick like their grandmother, grandfather, mother, father, sister, or brother?

I frowned and blinked, tears blurring my vision. "I know. But really, is there no set time for us to go? It would suck if it was planned for her to die right now in front of her grandson. He can't be more than four."

Our time is not predestined. As you hold your humanity in the palm of your hands, there are others that threaten that fragility. A tired driver, a texting teen, or rainstorm. A freak accident may occur because of a natural source. Avalanches are an act of nature, they occur. We know this, yet we ski. Skiing is not a disease. A flooded raging river is a part of nature. A car gets swept away but we still drive in bad weather. It is no one's fault, Grace. When our time comes, it is time. But will the human side of ourselves be at peace with it?

"I sure as heck wouldn't be." My right temple throbbed. The sun seemed hotter the longer we stood there. I couldn't see the woman but the people still standing around seemed calmer. "This sucks. That boy did not deserve this."

True, and if she dies, he will always remember her on this day. He will remember the people who rushed to help his grandma. And the fruit he picked will hold a special place in his heart.

The ambulance came to a stop in the grass only a few yards away. The attendants opened the back doors and dropped the gurney to the ground. The crowd parted and her son stood as the EMTs went to work.

I could see her again. She was on her back in the dirt. The Grammy Air machine whirred in spurts. It sounded like it was still pumping oxygen, but the tube had fallen away.

They loaded her onto the stretcher, a new oxygen tank placed between her knees and a fresh tube placed beneath her nose. Her son picked up her machine and started toward the market. "I'll get my son and meet you at the hospital."

The wail of the sirens faded, and the people disbursed. It took me a moment to realize I was standing alone.

"Do you think she'll make it?" I asked Summer.

I do not think, nor do I know. I am an angel, a guide for you to learn the importance of life, but to understand the beauty so that you touch as many beautiful people as you can. That is how you will live on after you pass, and how those connections will find their way back.

I believe her desire was for her grandson to remember her always. That desire is fulfilled because she made it so. I would not be surprised if she became his angel today. She may not manifest, but rather watch over him and wait for him until that day comes when he is an old man, ready to pass. This I know, Grace. She will be waiting.

Deep in my gut, I thought the worst, but in my heart, I had hope. I didn't care if her energy had mingled with the boy or mine or anyone else. I wanted that boy to have more time to say goodbye. I wanted the son to never look out at the strawberry patch and remember that his mother's last conscious moments were there.

Touch their lives, Grace. What can you do to connect? Ask yourself, how can I make a difference?

CHAPTER 6
PAYING IT FORWARD

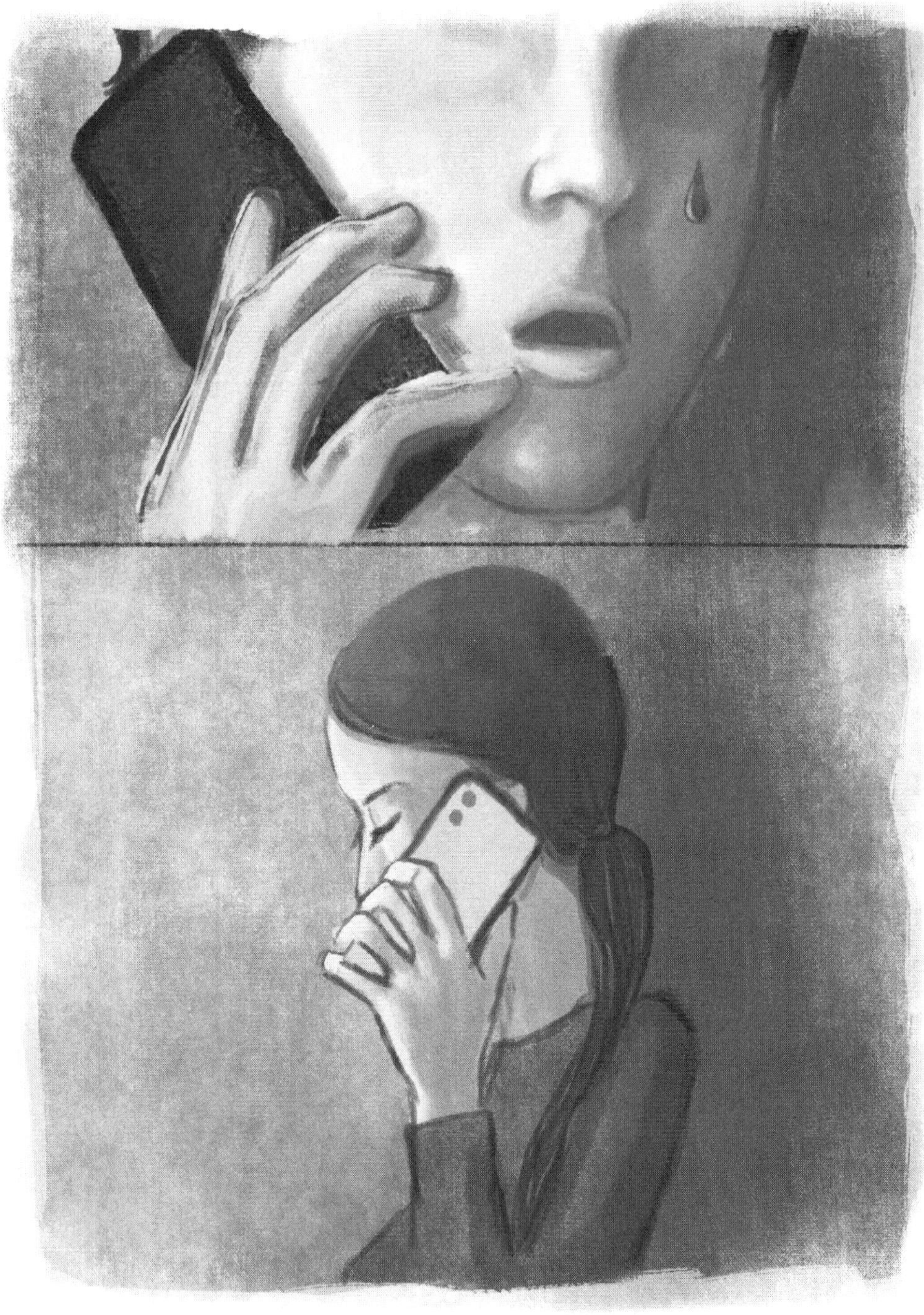

I took Summer's advice at the strawberry patch. I decided to call the strawberry patch phone number in hopes they knew the woman or at least could give me her contact information.

It felt awkward and I knew it would be a difficult call, but every piece of me needed to try. I itched to dial, but my husband urged me to give them some time. I waited until the end of the next day.

A young female voice answered.

"Good evening, my name is Grace. My family and I were strawberry picking yesterday and I had a lovely chat with a woman who was there with her son and grandson. A short while later, she collapsed and was taken away by ambulance. I was hoping you knew how I could get in touch with her family. I wanted to know how she's doing and if there is anything I could do."

"Oh, um. Let me get my husband," the young woman said.

A moment later a man's voice came on the line. "Hello?"

"Good evening, my name is Grace. I was there when the woman collapsed yesterday. I was wondering if you would know how to get in touch with her or her family."

There was a pause. "That woman is my mom."

"I'm so sorry. I didn't realize." It felt like an intrusion, but I had to know. It ate at me. I'd never felt like this before with such a strong need to find out. I hope this is what Summer had in mind when she urged me to do something. Maybe this is an angel's will.

"I was calling to see if she is okay and if I could do something for you or your family? As I mentioned to your wife, we had a lovely chat and I felt a strong connection to her."

"Ah, you're the lady with the kids who kept Connor busy. Thank you." He cleared his throat and paused. "My mom passed away at the hospital this morning." He cleared his throat again. "She regained consciousness briefly. Connor and the family were able to say our goodbyes. A short while later, she closed her eyes and was gone."

I heard a muffled cry, then a shuffle of the receiver.

"Hi, it's Cindy. Big Connor's wife. Thank you for calling. We appreciate your concern. You should be very proud of your kids. Little Connor asked if they might want his strawberries. He has plenty. His grandmother would help him pick while we ran the market."

Tears trailed down my cheeks. "Is there any way I can help? Maybe my kids and I could help at the market while you attend to the arrangements."

That's it, Grace. Summer's voice echoed inside me.

"Uh, I don't know," Cindy hesitated. "Your kids were so sweet with Connor, but we couldn't ask that."

"Do you need them to watch him? We can come to you."

"I couldn't ask that. I don't even know you." I could hear her cry.

"You don't need to ask. We'll be there tomorrow morning. Consider us volunteers at the market. We're strangers no more. Strangers are simply friends we haven't met yet." My voice sounded like a sci-fi character to me. My nerves had my brain jumbled, though I felt Summer inside me, coaxing me in some way.

"Okay," Cindy whispered. "Alright. And thank you, Grace."

"We need to touch as many lives as we can, Cindy. I am reaching out to touch yours. Maybe one day you will do the same when someone else needs it."

I hung up and turned around to see Summer sitting on the arm of the sofa. "I thought you were echoing inside me."

> I was. You are an angel here and now, Grace. You have a kind heart that is reaching out for a connection. Those connections will grow and bond. Your children are doing the same. As we transfer that energy, remember we leave a bit of ourselves.

Your kids have already imprinted on that child and you with his grandmother. The family will be waiting with anticipation, not even realizing what they need is that connection. You are the light in their time of darkness. They will never forget you.

"How do I transfer my energy if I don't know how?"

Just be there. Talk with them and show them what an outsider's love can do.

"I will, Summer."

The kids were at the store with their father, so I shared my plan in text speak. I got two thumbs up. "They're in," I smiled at her. "So, why did you stick around this time? Come to think of it, the first time you visited for two days also. Why not more often?"

I told you, your thoughts and memories called me. My energy is one with the fields and flowers, the bubbling streams, and the growing crab apples. I am in the sun and moon. When you weep or grieve, you call. For I am pulled by the intensity of your emotions. And I am kept here with you when you won't let me go.

"What do you mean? I let you go." I was puzzled because I had been happy after our visits. Why would she think I wasn't letting her go?

You pictured me in the woman's place. You pictured my children in the young boy's innocence. It has been more than a year since my passing and yet you picture me in the place of the dying and ill. Every time you encounter a similar situation, it will lead you toward believing it is familiar. But I ask you, Grace, is it? Is it familiar? Or is it a manifestation of your fears and experiences imprinting on your own memory to fulfill your desire to keep me with you?

I thought about that for a moment. Was I injecting my own emotions into the situations and people around me? Was what I thought a familiar reliving, or déjà vu, actually the act of not letting go of my dearest friend? I would have asked, but her figure had vanished from the kitchen.

I ran to the bedroom, grabbed my journal, and wrote *Déjà vu?* Because, in all honesty, I did not know when I would see Summer next. It could be in the fall or next Christmas. One thing for certain was that I had my family to help.

My question for Summer would have to wait.

CHAPTER 7
SHARING THE LOVE

"Are you excited?" I asked my son. It was graduation, the day parents all over the world celebrate their children's accomplishments. It is hard to believe their final year of school has come and gone. For me, the sound of *Pomp and Circumstance dredged* up feelings of nostalgia. I remember the flood of anticipation, the surreal moment walking across the stage and receiving my diploma. And here and now, I realize my own little bundle of joy is a young adult. *How did the time fly so fast?* I wondered.

I pictured my son, wrapped in a powder blue receiving blanket with tiny wooden blocks spattered around the fabric. His peach-fuzz-covered head so tiny I could fit it in my hand. Was that really the same young man sitting in the chairs before me, about to walk across the stage? I swore I wouldn't cry but tears wet my eyes. It was a happy day, and after graduation, we were going to Hibachi with the grandparents. The celebration was only beginning. Festivities for other graduates were planned throughout the summer, my son's included. And in two months he was leaving for his freshman college year.

Other mothers seemed to drift in and out of the moment. I suspected they, too, were experiencing the same feelings of nostalgia. I was lucky, my daughter still held my hand, and hugged me. I saw a few students who blew their mothers off. My eyes settled on a father and daughter, sitting next to each other facing the stage. The man's face looked worn and tired, his daughter stiff and straight-faced. She had the look of a teen who had experienced more than any child should. I got the sinking feeling that mom was not in the picture, and not by choice.

And for a brief moment, I thought about Summer's son. He was graduating the same day, but at a different high school, crossing a different stage. *Are her husband and kids sitting in the audience like the two across from me?*

I promised myself I was going to hold it together until I was alone. But sometimes we make promises that have no meaning. Why did I feel the need to weep alone? It wasn't what I wanted. Being there to see my son, I felt lucky and blessed. The milestones are all important and so are the small things. But this is the day every child shares a secret desire for their parents to be there in the audience, bursting with pride. Summer's son would not have his desire fulfilled. Chances were he felt joy because he was graduating and his dad was there to witness it, but nothing could take the place of his mom.

Summer*, if my memories are calling you, stop. I want you to go to your family. See your son. Be with him,* I thought. If she was going to manifest today, I wanted it to be with the person who wished she was there to share his special moment. I didn't feel or see her, but there was a soft breeze that picked up in the bleachers. My daughter's program blew from her hands and landed on my white high-heeled shoes. The last page faced upward; the others folded beneath in a strange but deliberate way. Two words, printed in large bold font read *Thank you!*

I was awestruck. It had been two years since our last encounter, yet today, that message just happened to land at my feet when I happened to make my heartfelt request. I was willing to bet it was a message from Summer. I felt the connection in my heart pulled and she answered.

I reached down and handed the program to my daughter. "I'm so proud and lucky to be here for you and your brother. I want you to know that. I'm the luckiest mom on the planet."

My daughter smirked, but the corner of her lip tilted up then spread into a full grin. "We're lucky too, Mom."

We share a deep parent-child relationship. I never wanted them to grow up thinking they were on their own. I fostered their growth and encouraged them to be independent, but I made sure they knew anytime they wanted or needed me, I would be there with open arms. A steady flow of weeping tears slid down my face. I was reminded of the tears that moistened my shirt during one of Summer's encounters several years back. I laughed at myself, *Were those angel tears?*

The band started to play *Pomp and Circumstance* and the graduates were lined up stepping in time from the sidelines. I pointed out that the school spread a green Astroturf carpet so they would not soil their dress shoes.

My husband, the one I could count on to alleviate heavy emotions with humor, touched my arm with his elbow. "They still have to walk on the grass to get to their chairs."

I shook my head and laughed aloud. Of course, he was right. It reminded me how much I loved him. He was a true half to my whole. And because of that, I wondered if he said it to alleviate his own pangs of nostalgia or give me a slap of reality and bring me back to graduation. It didn't matter because it accomplished both.

I held my daughter's hand, knowing that in a few years, she would be down there, preparing to walk across the stage. I took my husband's and daughter's hands in mine, and the three of us sighed. It was a special moment.

Summer had offered me a fresh look on life. I began noticing the small things and the big effects they had on me. The other day I was aware of the instant melt of my taut shoulders when I embraced my husband. It was only a fraction of an inch, but it was there, and I don't think he even knew. It was an involuntary acknowledgment of our love and the bond between us.

I gasped and glanced around. *Are you in my thoughts?* I asked Summer.

Always.

I watched my son walk across the stage, shake hands with the dignitaries, and receive his diploma. We clapped harder than we ever clapped before. We were a small family of mother, father, and sister, but we were proud, and we let it show.

And somehow having Summer in my thoughts lightened the weight on my shoulders. She came back.

CHAPTER 8
HOLD ONTO YOUR HUMANITY

I was sitting at the traffic light in City Center. The day was foggy, overcast, and humid. I hadn't seen or heard from Summer in over seven years. She became a piece of memory, someone I recalled from time to time when I needed to settle down and regroup. It seemed there were more of those days and nights recently.

The taxis and buses were maneuvering through the traffic, and pedestrians clad in raincoats with umbrellas were hopping over puddles and sloshing along the sidewalks. I noticed a white kitten dash from around the corner of the limestone building. A sinking feeling washed over me. I wanted to rush to it, sensing something bad was about to happen.

The light turned green, and I made my left turn, the same direction the cat was headed. I was too late. A flood of childhood memories bombarded me as I stopped the car and stared at the white, lifeless body. My Mittens met the same fate when I was in elementary school. I relived seeing her body from the school bus window on a dank, rainy spring day, much like today.

A horn beeped behind me, and I lurched the car forward with tears in my eyes.

"Damn, it," I yelled, hitting the steering wheel.

Easy there, Grace.

I turned to see Summer's haze seated beside me in the passenger seat. "It's been a while."

Remember time is neither great nor small. The kitten's life goes on.

"Yes, I suppose it does. I knew something was going to happen. I had the gut feeling you get, that sense of déjà vu." I glanced back at her. "I wrote it in my journal years ago to remind me to ask you the next time we visited. Is déjà vu like fortune telling? How could I know it would end this way for the poor little cat? Was it an angel or some other power that gave me that feeling?"

She turned her mist-shrouded face toward me and placed her hand over mine.

> My friend, this circumstance is not unique. The human mind finds ways to make predictions. In the world, there are few circumstances that are a one-time event. There are similar deaths, encounters, and celebrations. The memories you have are dredged up to the surface. You do see the future, but only what you have experienced or possess as known knowledge. If you never saw an animal hit by a car or heard of a tale that told of such, then your

foundational knowledge would create the scene which appeared to be a premonition. It is a feeling of having been there or done that, even though it has not happened. At some point in our human lives, we experience and learn.

Humanity is both beautiful and ugly. The truth is when you have a feeling inside you question its validity. I ask you, what difference does the validity of the question make? If something looks bad, or can end in an undesirable way, then we have an innate need to divert from the situation. We desire a pleasurable outcome, no matter the circumstance. You are human still. You want to save everyone and everything, but you cannot. It is cliché but there is no simpler way to explain why you have a loving heart. You seek pleasure in taking away the hurt of others. It is another reason why you are special.

Hold onto your humanity, Grace.

"I will." I glanced at her again. We were headed out of the city and back to my house. "Summer, where were you? I mean, you didn't come back. Do you know how long it's been?" I questioned if she knew it was seven years since our last visit. All the other visits she spoke about time as a measure of human moments, for lack of a better explanation. It was nearing a decade since we last spoke. What would an Angel do for that long?

> I watched over the kids, my husband, and you. There is no one place to dwell or go. I visit and become part of those whose lives I touched. I have watched you thrive after leaving the golden handcuffs of your corporate life. I wonder if the loss you had when I died has propelled you to make the changes you have? If so, I'm glad! How long has it been?

"Seven years, plus a few months. It was our first autumn visit." I smiled, hoping to take the sting away, if there was a sting. She had grown quieter with each visit. As she sat beside me on our trip back home, she didn't speak. Her blue haze was more of a pale yellow. Like sunlight shining on the upholstery, only it was raining. The clouds were thick, gray, and ominous. My friend was the manifestation of sunshine. But her quieted state had me puzzled. "Summer, what's wrong?"

> Have you thought about the things you want to do before you die? Things you can do only as a human.

"I guess. Why?" Goosebumps raised over my arms.

Her hazed form solidified into my friend enough for her to watch the fields pass by the window. The further west we traveled, the better the weather. The rain subsided, the clouds were lightening, and ahead of us was a patch of blue sky. She seemed to sigh or undulate in a rhythmic wave.

My cell phone rang, and I put my finger up to put our conversation on hold while I answered using the car speakers. "Hey, baby."

"Hi, mom. How far away are you?" my daughter asked.

"Maybe half an hour. Why?"

"I'm at the house. I brought the baby shower stuff including green and yellow decorations." She laughed, "I feel old-fashioned, not wanting to know the gender. But Sam and I think it's part of the fun."

"I'll be there soon. I can't wait to see. And there is nothing old-fashioned about being an excited mama and daddy. What's not old is planning your own shower. It's strange, but I love the fun we're having by doing it together."

"I'll let you go. Could you bring home some chicken wings? Love you, mom."

"You got it. Love you, too." I ended the call.

My daughter was due with her first child in October. It was a beautiful time, and she was happy. I was happy, her father and brother, too. Even her husband couldn't wait. For a moment I was lost from the conversation with Summer, and then the realness of her message hit me. What things did I want to do before I die? I wanted to be there for my daughter's labor and delivery. I wanted to be there every time if there were to be more than one. I wanted to walk down the aisle at my son's wedding alongside his fiancé's mother. I wanted to hold his hand when he was about to be a father. Did Summer have regrets?

"What human things are you asking me about?"

Like feeling and smelling the wind on a beautiful summer's day. She raised her cheeks skyward and closed her eyes.

I find myself trying to remember touching my daughter's cheek.

"Oh, Summer," I choked back instant tears. "I'm so sorry."

The taste of my son's lemonade, sour and sweet, while rocking on the porch with him by my side. Those things, Grace. I don't want to lose them.

I pulled over on the side of the road. Whether she could feel it or not, I reached out to hold her hand. It was such a simple gesture in life and felt so natural. I clasped her hand between mine in hopes of her feeling my warmth around her hand's light. There was a faint coolness which I had come to recognize as her being.

Help me remember. Being human can never be repeated.

She turned her face to me. I recognized the blue haze from her previous visits.

Show me.

CHAPTER 9
MEMORIES AND REMEMBRANCES

I arrived at the house with my daughter's chicken wings, but she was sound asleep on top of my bed, curled up like a kitten. I covered her with her favorite afghan, the one my mother made for her when she was just a little thing. I could tell she'd been in my hope chest looking through photo albums and pictures. I picked up the loose ones scattered around her and kissed her cheek.

I tiptoed down the stairs with all the photo albums I could carry. My daughter had decorations strewn across the kitchen and dining room, so I moved to the living room and dropped them on the coffee table. "Let me get us a cup of tea and we can talk."

Summer was lingering by the sofa, her form returned to the yellowish hue, brightened in the darkening room by the setting sun.

I prepared two mugs of water with tea bags and put them in the microwave to boil. I placed the hot mugs on a tray with my honey bear and creamer. I knew Summer liked her tea sweet and creamy.

"All set," I said as I poured the honey into our cups. "You always said the honey smells like springtime. When I close my eyes, I can see the flowers."

Summer came closer to the cup I slid toward her.

I poured the cream in and stirred. "I don't know what to do. If I'm being ridiculous for serving my best angel tea, then so be it. I'll do my darndest to keep your memories alive for you, Summer."

Thank you, Grace. I remember your tea.

I sat on the rug next to the coffee table, my back against the sofa, and sipped. I let the flavors roll over my tongue. "Do you remember the honey's sweet tang and the way the cream mingles with the bitter tea?"

I remember enjoying the flavors but cannot recall them.

I turned on the table lamp and opened one of the photo albums. The first page held images of when our kids had their first playdate. I held the album in my lap and pointed to a photo of our boys sitting in the sandbox together. "I remember when that was taken. They had so much fun, digging in the sand and sharing the same toy truck. Do you recall any of that day?"

Her haze was muted by the lamplight, but I could still make out her form. She ran her hand over the photos on the page. It didn't seem like she was able to concentrate on one specific photo as her link to her own humanity. I wanted to find a way to trigger her human side. I remember during our first visit she was holding on to the family she loved and how much she missed them. She hated watching her children grieve her loss. Now it was eleven years later, and she couldn't seem to remember their soft skin and those warm sunny days.

I never wanted to forget the way my daughter's face felt when I kissed her forehead or the way my son left scant wetness behind his quick kisses as he ran out the door. I flipped through the photo album looking for the pictures of Summer and her children. It didn't matter if she remembered me or my kids, but her own? I couldn't accept that.

I found a picture of Summer with her children, all smiling, sitting on a picnic blanket. We had met at the park on a picture-perfect spring day. I pulled it from the sleeve and sat it next to the tea. I found another where she was kissing her daughter's hand, a show of love from the mom who had a princess in her midst. And then there was one with her son clinging to her as they approached Santa in the mall. He hugged her so tight, he had her hair in his clasp along with her bright red Christmas sweater.

She was right. Humanity had millions of moments that could not be recreated. Perhaps that also fit in with my questions about déjà vu. The possibility existed for so many similarities in life, but none were a perfect re-creation. Each moment was unique to our individual human selves.

"Summer, take a look at these." I tapped the photos by her tea. I sipped mine and thought of how to explain the flavors.

"This tea was your favorite. Unless it was summer and then you liked genuine homemade sweet tea. Do you remember?"

I remember sweet tea. It made me smile because it reminded me of home, the South where I grew up. I can't remember the flavor, but I remember my mother pouring it into tall glasses over ice.

She looked at the photos. Her haze hovered in a concentrated mass over each. She settled on the one with the three of them in the park.

I know I loved them. They were everything to me.

"Maybe what you feel is not the same as when you were human, Summer, but that love is keeping you here. You watch over them. You stay with them. Who says that is not love? If you ask me, your love was so deep, it followed you into the afterlife and survived your transition. This is your first time being an angel. How do you know that instead of feeling, you exist because of the strength of those emotions? I don't think you're losing your humanity. I think you evolved your human side. Because right here, right now, I see a mother's love."

The yellow hue faded in and out. I turned off the lamp to see her better.

I don't want to lose my human memories. You tell me they were happy then and that I was happy. Life is timeless and joyful now but it's harder to remember the times before this.

"Then why are you looking at these same pictures over and over again? Perhaps this is your known knowledge, as you put it. And why shouldn't you look? They were wonderful times, and these are wonderful memories. I will make sure to keep these pictures out. This way any visit we have will be your connection to your human life. And I will have sweet tea, whether it be spring, summer, winter, or fall."

Thank you, Grace.

"Thank me next time."

Her light and hue vanished, and I was left sitting alone.

My daughter rounded the corner from the stairs and stopped at the entrance to the living room. "Why are you sitting in the dark?"

"No reason." I reached over and turned the lamp back on. "Find any photos for the shower?"

She pulled one from her sweater pocket. It was one where she and I were seated at the same coffee table having tea. "I thought of this one. It's so us." She pointed at the table. "Maybe it's a sign."

I stood up and wrapped my arms around her, pulling her pregnant belly into mine. "I love you, kiddo. Don't you ever forget that."

She squeezed me back. "I love you more." She stepped back, "Is the extra cup of tea for me? And what's with the pics of Aunt Summer?"

I laughed, "You know, I thought I'd have a conversation with an angel. What a better angel to hope for than Aunt Summer? My daughter's going to have a baby. Why wouldn't I share?"

She lifted the cup of tea and took a sip. "Don't ever change, Mom."

"I don't plan to."

CHAPTER 10
SLIPPING AWAY

Life has its ups and downs, and it is up to us if we let it keep us at our lowest. When my husband got the call from the cardiologist, I was prepared. I already had practice with Summer before she died. I knew he was on borrowed time since his first heart attack. After the bypass surgery, the doctor told us his heart was weakened and it was only a matter of time before it would give out.

The kids and I were lucky to have him with us as long as we did. He got to see his two precious grandchildren our daughter brought into the world, and he stood as best man at his son's wedding. The happy couple decided to choose the two people closest in their lives to stand up for them. My daughter-in-law chose her mom, and my son chose his father. It was beautiful and new.

"Everything these kids do is unconventional," he said.

"That's what our parents said about us," I retorted.

He squeezed my hand and coughed. "I'm ready. It'll be good to take a long nap."

"Oh, stop. Besides, I told you, when your time comes, I'll be watching for you every time I look up at the stars or see the sun glinting through the windows." I had to stop before I lost control.

I was doing well. He lasted a long time with heart disease, and surgeries, longer than his doctors predicted. I knew he was tired, not so much tired of fighting to win, but just fatigued. I was prepared, but in truth, none of us are ever ready.

I left his hospital room to wander down to the cafeteria. There were too many options when all I wanted was to grab something to keep me alive. I grabbed a ginger ale and a chocolate chip scone before heading to the atrium. I liked to go there during the late-night hours when no one else was there. It was a place I could clear my thoughts. I found a sofa in a back corner, curled up, and sipped my soda. It was reminiscent of the days I visited with Summer. They were feelings I don't want to relive.

Grace.

I glanced around for Summer's hue, but there was no sign of her. "Summer?" I whispered.

I am with you.

"I don't know if I can do this again, Summer. I'm not okay." I tossed the scone on the side table and swigged the ginger ale. "I'm losing him. Each day he's more tired, and I can feel him slipping away. His eyes are just slits tonight. He can't even open them to look at me. I sent the kids home for a change of clothes, but they'll be back soon."

Remember, he is not leaving you. Only the version of him you know. He will stay with you always. Will the kids stay with you until it is his time?

"They want to, but my daughter needs to be with her kids. Granted her oldest is thirteen, but I would never ask her to stay. He doesn't want the attention either."

I wasn't sure the last was true. My husband was a good man, but like a lot of men, his emotions didn't always come through his words. He was a man of action. Did he want them to stay? It was a good guess the answer was 'yes' regardless of what he said.

They are not children anymore, Grace. If they want to stay, they should. He will pass and all of you will take on his energy. Be with him. Hold his hand and sing to him the way you sang to me. Show him your love, your humanity, and encourage the kids to do the same. It is through them that he will live on, and when he makes his transition, you will notice. It is a gift I have given you. The knowledge to notice an angel's light.

"I know you said that, and I am ready to let him rest. But I am not ready to be without my partner. The best father and loving husband. Again, I could say it isn't fair, but I remember your answer from many years ago. It still doesn't take away my pain."

Allow yourself time to grieve, Grace. Crying is a must. I do not remember sadness, but I have memories of crying. In some way, it makes me feel whole, knowing that I shared my love with special people. In our human state we love our children and relations because they are part of us, but our spouses are chosen. They are not a birthright or gift; they are choices that we make to complete our lives.

When Ben passes, you will be left alone. I told you before to hold onto your humanity. This is one of those times that your humanity is vulnerable. You will want to turn off your emotions and shut out the world. You can't let that happen. The act of shutting it out would be unfair, not only to you, but to him, your kids, and the rest of those in your world. You are not alone, Grace.

I got up from the couch and headed back to his room. The nurse stationed outside his room gave me a smile that said she understood. I wondered if she ever went through losing the love of her life. Or perhaps she was sympathizing with me the way she did with all the spouses and partners under her care. Either way, it was appreciated. I needed to feel a connection to someone in the living world.

I sat on the edge of my husband's bed. His breathing was softer. I didn't want to leave, but I was exhausted. The hospital was kind enough to lend me a pillow and blanket to sleep in the recliner in his room. After listening to Summer's advice, I decided I wanted my kids to stay. I was afraid to be alone and afraid to let him die.

***

My son came in first. He carried a plastic shopping bag stuffed with my clothes. His hair was damp and combed, and it looked like he shaved. "If this is the last time dad sees me, he's going to remember me as someone to be proud of."

"He's always been proud of you," I whispered. "He loves you with all his heart."

Sharp heel clicks on the tiled floor let us know my daughter had arrived. She stepped into the room dressed in a green plaid dress, wearing black heels, her hair pinned back. "I want Dad to know that you will never be alone. We will take care of you, Mom. He deserves to be at peace and that won't happen if he doesn't believe you will be alright. He wants us all to be taken care of and that's what we'll do for each other."

"You know he loves you with all his heart, right?" I asked her.

"Yes, Mom. And we'll be right here by both your sides until the end."

You have good kids, Grace. Let them take care of you. It is how they will show their love and cope with losing their father. When a loved one dies, it is hard to be rejected. Don't be the one to reject their offers. You are their mother. You took care of them. It is time that they get to reflect some of that care and compassion back to you.

Think about the time you made tea and chose photos for me to remember my human life. You impressed upon me the transition of love is that which I express through my visits. Why then, do you insist on refusing to accept their transition from children to caregivers? Is there no greater joy in humanity than to help another? And when that other is your own mother, the joy knows no bounds.

"I'm glad you're both here," I hugged my children, and we clustered our chairs together by his bedside. They were blessings beyond any a heart could find in a time of need, and mine needed them. My husband needed them. "I'm not ready to let him go." I said and sobbed.

My husband squeezed my hand and opened his eyes. He looked at all three of us. We reached forward and held the same hand binding us all together.

"I love you," I cried.

And he took his last breath. His heart was at rest. The monitor droned a steady beep and the nurse rushed in. We each took turns kissing his hand and cheek before we had to leave. I hoped beyond hope that Summer was right, that my husband took his first big leap into his new life. And that he would cling to his humanity as I hoped I would cling to mine.

I hoped that she might even be there on the other side waiting for him. Even if it was only to say, “Hello.”

CHAPTER 11
CELEBRATE LIFE

They say that learning to live without your life partner is a death like no other. Those people are right. But there is so much more to losing a partner. It is a transition of its own. Everything you say, do, think, and feel changes. You change because you are a manifestation of the two of you.

One might even say it is a rebirth. You relearn how to live without your other half. Maybe Summer will enlighten me on that whenever she decides to visit next.

All I knew was I was alone, without being alone. And I was sad while being happy. My son and his wife moved in with me and their antics made me smile from ear to ear. But as many a widow and widower know, that smile covers a deep sadness. For me, watching their antics brought on reminiscence which led to more grieving and the daily reminder that I was alone.

Yes, I wasn't living alone, there were moments I couldn't share with my kids or my friends. If you have lived through such a loss, then you understand. I think what I missed most was being someone else's *person*.

I sat in my room with Summers' pictures lined on my dresser. I kept my husband's side of the bed neat and slept on the small section that was mine since we were married. I was lucky to have such a good man in my life. I kept his spot for him, just in case he did visit.

I blinked at my reflection in the mirror. "When did my hair get so gray? And where did those wrinkles come from?" I asked no one in particular.

> Are you asking for real? Because that is beyond the knowledge of an angel. I already told you time has no measure in the afterlife. We are where we are supposed to be, Grace.

Summer's blue haze settled in the space between my vanity stool and the end of the bed.

> Look up at the stars, and you will see us all. Walk barefoot in the grass and you will collect the energy from thousands of ancestors who graced your path. Alone is a frame of mind. Humanity requires relationships. If you do not share with the people in those relationships, then they will not build their foundational knowledge to go forward when they reach the milestones and obstacles that you have already conquered. It is another beautiful part of being alive. Embrace your grief, but do not let it blind you. There is beauty in remembering. It is also a way of keeping Ben alive. Even if it is within your

own heart. His energy and love flowed into each of you. Not everyone gets to have that moment.

I will visit again tomorrow. We will walk in the morning, and you will tell me about all that I am missing.

***

I awoke to the sun shining in my window. It reflected off the vanity mirror and I thought about Summers' visit. She said she was coming in the morning. I was motivated to rush downstairs, eat breakfast, and sip my coffee while I waited.

It was half-past ten when I finished my bagel. I washed the cream cheese knife and wiped the counter before pouring a second cup. My son and daughter-in-law were at work, so I was left to chatter with my beloved angel.

"Summer? Are you around?" I looked up at the ceiling and then again toward the living room. "Summer, it's morning."

It is. Take off your slippers and leave your coffee.

"Ah, a grounding moment." I kicked off the slippers and gulped a few swallows of coffee before setting the cup in the sink. "All set."

Follow me.

Summer manifested into herself, the clearest I had seen yet. She was a pale white hue with the image of her human self within. That figure floated outside to the backyard all the way to the meadow. I followed.

Lie down, Grace.

I did as she directed. I was barefoot, laying in the lawn. The glory surrounding me took my breath away. The sun accented the green treetops, and white puffy clouds drifted across the sky. I felt the occasional breeze refresh the skin between my toes, and the hairs on my arms. The grass was soft and cool. It smelled like summer, dirt, and flowers from distant gardens. I closed my eyes and inhaled, savoring the wonder of it all.

This is what it means to be human, Grace. I lost this, not the moment, but the enjoyment. It is a distant memory now.

Give yourself permission to enjoy. When you lose your loved ones, you deny all the pleasure that makes being human worth the experience. I want to remember the grass. You have been trying to prevent the creation of new memories you know your husband will not share with you. Allow yourself to experience life while you still have your humanity, Grace. He is all around you, in the grass, the wind, the trees, and blossoms.

The energy and love you shared will bring him to you. Feel the sun warm your skin. The kiss of a summer's day is filled with our energy–all of us. He is not gone, but instead, moved on. Remember when I told you love draws us to our loved ones?

"Yes," I said.

When you enjoy and celebrate life and your humanity, you celebrate the lives that were lost to you, then you remember. But the beauty lies in the connection you make with what they have become. The interpersonal energy is here. Accept what you cannot see, and do not understand. Know that it is part of who we are and who we were. The stars did not disappear because the sun rose to give you a new day. They are still there. Do you see?

"I do. We are of the universe even when it is hidden by the sun's light of day. When night falls, we get a glimpse of what lies beyond our small world. The wonder should not diminish because we can't see it. It should increase because we know in our hearts what is there. And even though we can't see it, no matter how hard we try, we must believe that all our loved ones transitioned to all that is. We are not bound after death. We are released."

I glanced around at the symphony of greens in the grasses and the leaves. The array of colors complimented the robin egg blue sky. I shielded my eyes from the sun and raised my chin to feel its warmth. The cool earth beneath me contrasted with the emotions I felt within.

> You want to accept the warmth on your skin, but you don't want to stop feeling the cool grass on your back. My question to you is why do you have to refuse one to enjoy the other? What makes one more important or enjoyable?

"Why do we struggle to make ourselves choose? Does it matter to anyone but us, as individuals? Unless I tell someone, they won't know I debate with myself over feelings, reactions, and decisions. It is unnecessary stress. But how do you overcome the urge?"

> Choose not to choose. You must overcome your struggles by accepting all those moments as a part of the experience. There is no higher power or greater influence dictating which way you should go. Choose to live and then live in the moment.

I lay in the grass for a while longer. I stretched my arms and stroked the soft blades. Each one was alive. It took the energy of the sun and turned into food. How was that lost on me? No human could feed on the energy from the sun, but it was the life force that feeds all that sustains us here on Earth. When the sunshine hits the plants around us, there is a transference of energy.

"If the transference of energy is accepted as fact, and we know this through science, then why was it so hard for me to accept the energy of all those I have loved?" This private moment in the field proved to me that our grounding was part of making the connection.

I turned to Summer for confirmation, but she was no longer there. I made a mental note to ask her next time: How does grounding bridge our connections?

CHAPTER 12
RECOGNIZING THE PRESENCE

A number of years passed since my last visit with Summer. I was nearing my seventieth birthday. I made a habit of going barefoot in the grass and found new places to lie back and take in nature's wonders.

I had my lemon water with a handful of blackberries for breakfast. I wore my white shorts and pink top, ready to do my Sun Salutations. I even taught my daughter-in-law and daughter to practice these daily routines. I discovered it was in the early morning with the sun on my face lying on the bare grass that I felt free and alive. It was invigorating.

For some unknown reason, today I wanted to see Summer. It was a long time since I yearned for one of our talks, but I had many epiphanies over the years. I wanted to share my newfound knowledge with her.

"Summer, are you around?"

I stepped outside and started my routine on the lawn. A few small birds, finches maybe, scattered when I reached skyward. I was disappointed because Summer didn't pop in as quickly as she had in the past. I felt a heartsick gnawing unease, the kind that disquiets your mind to the point where you lose focus of all else.

I am here, my friend.

I straightened up and saw her golden glow against the lilac tree that I planted next to my new potting shed. "Thank you, Summer."

She looked puzzled.

You called, with your heart. I am a memory away. You've changed.

"I'm getting old," I laughed.

She smiled.

"Let's say I'm more grounded than I used to be."

You found a way to reconnect. It did well by you.

"Yeah, about that. I've had a question about connections and why you aren't always around."

She remained in her sunlit haze by the bush.

I decided to move closer. "I guess I really want to know how I can tell when you are here. I don't always see signs when I need you. Did I lose the ability of feeling you?"

Grace, I am always around you. All you must do is listen, inside. You must open your heart. When you sleep at night, I am in your dreams. But those you do not recall. When you smell the scent of my favorite flowers and sip sweet tea, you think of me. Yet you don't realize I am there. I am everywhere.

There are connections angels make with the living. It can be through dreams which we share, a touch of reassurance, or a scent that reminds you of me. It is your humanity that recognizes these connections, but you feel vulnerable still. That vulnerability leads you away from me. You wait for me to let you know I am here when I never left. My energy surrounds and has no boundaries.

I have come to you as partial and full appearances. But there are more ways that I have guided you. Think about the notions you've experienced before choosing the better path. Those are common ways for communication to come through. Apprehension and second-guessing are guides to help you find your best solution. The question is: Do you stop to ask why you feel those notions? Did you ever think that I might be nearby?

"No." How many times did she try to connect with me? I was too busy connecting with the earth and concentrating on moving on, to realize that I was ignoring the person, the angel, that set me on the path to live. "All those times, I closed my eyes and saw you. Was that you or me?"

It depends. If you thought of me with purpose, then it was you. The others would be me reaching out to you. Have you ever thought about me when you hear my favorite song? Do you ever sing the way you did before I passed? Have you felt the relief of life drift through you when you plant your seeds? I am here, beside you.

I tried to remember all the times I thought about her. The few times I had to pick up the pictures that were jarred from the vanity when I closed the door too hard or bumped into it when vacuuming. They were all photos of Summer with her children. I had put them there to remind her of her humanity, but I didn't let myself open to her presence. When those photos dropped to the floor, I picked them up and put them back. I used the opportunity to run the dust rag over the surface where they sat. I was more annoyed than awestruck because I had to readjust and take a few moments from my cleaning or bedtime routine to replace the same frames, over and over again.

"I'm sorry, Summer. I never meant to ignore you or shut you out."

I do not feel ignored, Grace. I want you to know I am here, but which path to choose is up to you. If it feels wrong, then trust your feelings. Tread with caution as you venture forward with decisions that don't sit right. Make your decisions with your heart in mind. Chances are good that I am offering my voice to you. But do not apologize for not heeding or listening. It does not affect me as there is no good or bad way to accept your angel's communication.

The most important part is that you recognize my presence. It's up to you to decide if you want to accept me.

"I always want to accept you, Summer. My life changed when I met you in life, and then again when we reconnected after your death. I hate that I've been blind to the years I thought you left. Is it because I disappointed you that you manifested again to prove yourself to me?"

I do not feel anger, hate, or resentment. All those feelings left in my angelic transition. There is no ill-feeling or emotion within me. I do not go off and weep, because I have no sadness or woe. My sorrows have melted away with my form. When you realize I am here, I answer.

"So, when I see the butterflies skipping over the lilacs is it you?"

I am in those special moments you choose to see me, Grace. If a unique occurrence appears to you, then you are witnessing a sign that I am by you. It will pick up your spirits when you are sad or in need. And it will bring you hope when you have none. The rarest instances of beauty are those in which I come to you.

I settled back on the grass and crossed my legs. There was no need to apologize. After all, our conversation was an acknowledgment of my closure to her. If she needed to guide me, then I needed to look for her directions. When the time came for our next encounter, I would be ready. But until then, did I have to wait for her answers?

Maybe the best thing to do was to question everything and think: *What would Summer do?*

CHAPTER 13
NEW PERSPECTIVES

We all know that from the day we are born our time is limited. I chose to remain close to those whom I loved with all my heart. It seemed to be the one common theme that Summer repeated through our years conversing across our different realms.

I decided to search my heart and take notice of all those times she appeared. Every day, I saw her face in the photos and took a moment to pause and reflect on her life before and after death. I began celebrating her death day with honey buns and sweet tea. I wanted to feel the connection we shared and treasure every sign as a gift.

Connections to my dear angel became vivid. I no longer waited to see a strange hue that became her visage. Instead, I thought about her in fleeting moments and smiled at the sky. I took to celebrating my life, too. I went to dinner and visited places I had never been. Through my experiences, I knew Summer's influence lived on. I felt complete and whole venturing beyond my normal life. I was retired for years and started to live again.

I had amassed the means to take my children and their families with me on excursions that made my heart swell with joy. Each grandchild's giggle and twinkle in my children's eyes delighted me to the core. I do believe in those special moments their own angels were visiting them. I only hoped it was their father or my mom, or perhaps my dad. There were a lot of wonderful people who graced my life and if they were there to be angels to my children, I would be blessed.

The delighted young lives who sat with me at dinner and held my hands during walks in the park, I imagined were the work of angels. I often wondered if children were more open to their inner angels. They laughed so often and lived with innocence and hearts free of doubt. Or maybe they didn't need angels, as they were providers of joy and wonder on their own.

I added a new photo to my vanity, one my daughter framed for me. It was one from my wedding, and my husband and I were surrounded by our parents, grandparents, and other deceased aunts and uncles. It made me smile every time I remembered something about someone in the picture. But it also signaled to me that maybe my time had come.

Summer said that when someone passed, they transferred their energy to those with them. I had a serious conversation with my children about what I wished for at the end of my life. They knew, if I had a choice, I wanted to die at home in my bed with the dearest things in my life near me, holding my hands. And I wanted to feel those things that linked me to them so that I would remember them. Regardless of whether I would remember, I was determined to try.

The last doctor visit wasn't filled with fun jokes. He spoke about a leaking valve and how with someone my age, replacement surgery was not worth the risk. He figured I had six months.

Of course, the kids were upset. My daughter could not stop crying and I cried with her. For I loved my life and all the people in it. I wasn't ready to let go.

Summer showed me the way to find the silver lining on difficult days. She was with me when I stood in the rain and felt thousands of droplets wash over my face. I knew they came from the oceans and lakes far and near, and every drop was part of the energy of life. I learned to appreciate every moment and grasp my humanity. The doctors may have numbered my days, but I was going to pack them with as much life as my heart could hold.

***

The months went by quicker than I could live them. I found myself laying on my bed one beautiful summer evening.

My daughter came in and lay next to me as she often would when she was a child and wanted to talk. We spoke a little about what the grandkids were up to and what plans she and her hubby had for their upcoming holiday and then there was a long pause. She said, "Mama, are you afraid to die?

I realized at that moment, that I had no fear, only peace. I shared with her the peace I felt and said, "Honey, I have lived such a blessed life. I have done all the things I wanted to do and more. I'm ready to go home to my father." We both cried but they were happy tears.

Later that week my son arranged a family reunion via Zoom with my sisters and brother and extended family. They sang my favorite song to me, a family favorite that we sang at my Grandfather's funeral, "You Are My Sunshine."

Their rendition ended and I said, "Well, that should do it!" I thought what a great thing to be sung into heaven by my family. God wasn't quite ready for me that day, but a few days later, I woke unable to lift my arm. I called to my son. He didn't answer. I rolled from the bed and clasped the side table with my working arm. My heart raced, as I fumbled to the vanity mirror. The left side of my face drooped. "Damn it."

I sat back on the bed and reached for my old journal on the nightstand. With as much strength as I could muster, I threw it to the floor in an effort to get attention. I needed someone to hear me. I'd read that a stroke causes the sufferer to think they are speaking when they aren't. I hoped my journal would do the talking for me.

I heard footsteps rush upstairs. My son and daughter-in-law appeared, followed by my daughter. She sat next to me and drew me into an embrace. I fought to remain calm. "I think I had a stroke."

My son was already dialing 911.

***

I learned they would send me home to rest. It was an aneurism, a slow bleeder that caused the stroke. My heart was still going, weak but chugging along. My daughter took over my care and my son became my advocate. I was lucky because my speech wasn't impacted but the mobility on my one side never came back.

They hadn't heard me call that day but throwing my journal on the floor alerted them I was in trouble. We agreed that would be my signal if I was ever alone and needed them to come.

When you think you have time, you don't. I would have liked the other two months the doctor promised. But those two months were not part of my path.

I gaze at the photos that fill the surface of my vanity and dresser. They are filled with the faces of my loved ones. I believe I was drawn to them that day and they gave me the strength and the time to say my good-byes.

CHAPTER 14
WALK WITH ME

"Summer, can you hear me?"

I stepped out of the dark toward my angel. But she no longer had the familiar golden blue hue. She was an embodiment of herself, my old, dear friend. Her smile was as bright as I remembered. I was in a dream, lifelike yet surreal.

"I've missed you," I said.

I've been here. And now I am waiting.

"What are you waiting for, Summer?"

I think you know. We've shared a lot over the years. It's time for you to put those chats to use. Your pain will go away, along with the anxiety you have for your health. All those worries will be left behind.

She lay beside me on my husband's side of the bed, her head on the pillow.

Take my hand, Grace.

I took her hand. It was soft and warm. "I can feel you," I said. Tears dripped down the sides of my temples. "Why can I feel you? I tried so many times in the past."

Shhh.

She smiled, a reassuring smile, and entwined our fingers.

You have company. Your children are here.

I turned my head toward the window. The sheer white curtains filtered the bright shining sun that warmed me from head to foot. My son and daughter shared my hand, each holding a couple of fingers. I was weak, but not too weak to smile at them and gaze upon their tear-streaked faces. "I will always be with you," I whispered.

"We love you, Mom," they whispered back.

I gave them a reassuring smile filled with love. We all knew my time had come.

I'd lived eighty-two wonderful years. I had children, grandchildren, friends, and neighbors who loved me. The sweet family from the farmer's market became lasting friends who promised to look after my own loved ones when I was gone. The gesture was kind and reassuring. I had grown a thriving business following my exit from corporate America so many years ago that would create a legacy for my family for generations. These things settled my mind. I knew I was leaving my family in a better place than when I started. I had become a life long-learner after the loss of Summer and believed I had used all the gifts God had given me to live my best life.

I was the matriarch and had to pass the torch. I was on my way to the transition Summer described to me over the years. I knew she was with me before I saw her. She kept her promise, and she was here.

Summer tugged my hand.

It is time my friend. Close your eyes and rest. Let go of all your sadness, your fears.

I did as she told me. I released the grief from my mother's death. She had passed a short time before I lost Summer. I freed the memory of sitting by my father's bedside and stroking his brow after he took his last breath. I surrendered the memory of my dear sweet husband's passing that left me empty, sad, and heartbroken. The grandma in the strawberry field no longer haunted my vision.

I was at peace with my children, and they knew it was my time. I felt them sitting beside me; my daughter's soft hands and my son's moist kisses gave me comfort. My grandbabies kissed my cheeks, but I wasn't sure when.

I turned to Summer. I could see her face. "How long have I been here? The in and out. I don't remember sleeping."

Time has no meaning now, Grace. When you awake, you will be one with the stars. A piece of you will stay within your children, but you will soar.

"How will I know what to do? I don't want to leave." I gasped but there was no air. "Summer? I'm not ready. I have so many questions."

But you are. And you will have your answers. You will also have the opportunity to share the answers with others left here on Earth if you choose. Remember the Earthly world is not ours. The heavenly world is your eternal home. She squeezed my hand a bit tighter, and the questions stopped. There was blackness and quiet–a peaceful space.

Then my dear angel's voice broke the silence.

Walk with me, Grace. A new world awaits.

EPILOGUE

Letting go of loved ones doesn't mean we forget. It means letting them live on in peace and love. When Summer stayed with Grace it was a sign of true friendship and guidance. It was a special time that allowed Grace to experience the fullest, richest life that reached beyond family and the world she thought she knew. Grace's open heart brought peace to a grieving family while forming a lasting friendship that carried forth until her death. As she learned, opening her heart to love and acceptance enriched her life free from the boundaries of her human existence.

At the same time, love for her friend was the bonding element that called to her. Their connection brought her closer to home by showing her what it meant to feel joy, even if she could no longer experience what she had left behind.

Sometimes love is the way and guides us in life and death.

Acceptance is ours to find.

A note from our author Lisa

My friendship with Elizabeth forever changed the way I look at life. She taught me so many things. How to be a better daughter, a better friend, a better mother, a better wife, a more confident child of God. She was my best friend, my confidante, my role model, my example of what a godly woman is. Elizabeth was my insides, she was my guts, my confidence, and one of my greatest joys.

I've asked many of our friends through the years, "How in the world were we so lucky to be chosen as this woman's friend?" And she had many best friends as I think we are meant to have. To have spent a portion of our lives feeling her unconditional love and watching and learning from her deeply wise self was a true gift from our Heavenly Father. My prayer for all of you is that you have an Elizabeth in your life and if not yet, find one. Or even better, be an Elizabeth to someone else. Blessings to you all in this amazing life journey and I hope our paths cross again one day soon!

THE AUTHOR

Lisa Williams

Lisa is a recovered corporate executive who woke up one morning and realized she couldn't remember the last time she had learned something new. She started the mission at Lisa Williams Co, "To empower, equip and inspire one million people to hire themselves," after the loss of her mom and her best friend Elizabeth in the span of 10 months. Her certainty that God can use all things for good, fueled her through her grief and helped open her eyes to the many gifts God still had planned for her life.

Lisa and her kingdom-driven tribe help others step into their God-Gifted purpose with a bigger mission to create a group of "7 figure givers." She found her own financial freedom at 47 years old and did this working for someone else. Imagine the lives that can be impacted by teaching others to "generate in order to be generous!"

Lisa is a Certified Approval Addiction Coach, Wealth Educator and America's Business Matchmaker. She teaches people how the addiction of approval from others holds us all back in life and business. By overcoming this addiction, embracing financial education and gaining the skills to create multiple income streams, we can achieve the time and money freedom we all crave!

Lisa's next chapter has her locking arms with an overwhelming abundance of like minded friends. Good people, doing good things as life-long learners!

You can catch up with Lisa on her socials here:

https://lisawilliamsco.com/

Instagram -
https://www.instagram.com/lisa_williams_co/

Facebook
https://www.facebook.com/lisa.wiesewilliams

LinkedIn
https://www.linkedin.com/in/lisa-williams-a148588/

Pinterest
https://www.pinterest.com/lisawilliamsdreambuilder/_created/

YouTube
https://www.youtube.com/channel/UC9QsuhU8GjKszZ0FjtYzVJw

Calendar
https://calendly.com/lwilliamsrevolution